In the same series
At the Bottom of the Garden
At the Cinema
Football

First published 2015 by order of the Tate Trustees
by Tate Publishing, a division of Tate Enterprises Ltd,
Millbank, London SW1P 4RG
www.tate.org.uk/publishing

Originally published in French as *Poka & Mine. Le réveil*
Text and illustrations by Kitty Crowther
© l'école des loisirs, Paris 2005
This English edition © Tate Enterprises Ltd 2015
English translation by Ann Drummond in association with First Edition
Translations Ltd, Cambridge, UK © Tate Enterprises Ltd 2015

A catalogue record for this book is available from the British Library
ISBN 978-1-84976-244-1
Distributed in the United States and Canada by ABRAMS, New York
Library of Congress Control Number applied for

Printed in Italy by Grafiche AZ

Kitty Crowther

POKA & MIA

Wakey-wakey

TATE PUBLISHING

"Wake up, Poka!
It's a nice day outside."
"Hmm!" replies Poka.

"Come on, Poka!"
"Hmm!"

"Stay there…"

"Look what I've brought you."

"Here's your coffee, Poka.
I put in two sugars,
just the way you like it.
Nice, eh, Poka?"

"Have you finished, Poka?"
"Hmm! Nearly."

"You know what?
I'm going to get dressed."

"Whoosh!"

"The red one or the blue one?"

"The red. And the red trousers."

"There we go!"

"Oh no! Poka!
You're still asleep!"

"Me? Not at all!
Look, I'm ready."

"Come on, let's go to the pond."

"I love this spot," says Poka.
"What do you think, Mia?"

"   "
 . . . .